15
Ireland

To: Jackie

Enjoy the tour!

Best wishes

Love

visit in Ireland!

The Wise Owl Storybook

Jerry Mulvihill

Thank you ...

The remarkably talented Gerardine Cooper Sheridan, for bringing to life
my vision for each story and creating another stunning cover.

Eoin O'Brien, for revising and editing the stories.

Tina Counihan and all the team at Killarney Printing,
for allowing me the freedom to take this book in my own direction
and for working hard to make it a reality.

Joe Keogh, Vincent Cashman and the Coolwood Bird Sanctuary,
for letting me photograph and interact with their beautiful owls.

My whole family, for encouraging and supporting the book,
for your great ideas and your passion for what I do.

ISBN: 978-0-9574347-0-7

A cip catalogue for this book is available from the National Library.

Printed in Ireland
by Killarney Printing Ltd.

Author

Jerry Mulvihill

www.jerrymulvihill.com

www.facebook.com/jerrymul

Cover-art & Illustrations

Gerardine Cooper Sheridan

Editor

Eoin O'Brien

Printed by

Killarney Printing Ltd.

Sponsor

www.kerrybogvillage.ie

www.facebook.com/kerrybog

The Wise Owl

igh upon a tall oak tree, nestled amongst the leaves, perches a wise owl. She is known far and wild in the animal kingdom. Her glowing orange eyes have seen many things, and are full of knowledge. She is kind and generous, offering sound advice to those in need.

One day, a tired fox arrived at the tall oak tree. "Are you there, Owl?" He asked with a sigh.

"Hello, Fox," said the owl. "What can I help you with?"

The fox looked up at the owl with a relieved smile. "I need your help. I have just been chased through the forest by a pack of dogs. I barely escaped. This is the second time in the past week. They are getting faster. What can I do?"

The wise owl blinked her eyes slowly, deep in thought. She shuffled along the branch, closer to the fox. "Here is my advice, Fox," she said in a husky voice. "The next time they chase you, you must lead them off the trail. You are faster than them, so you can trick them. When you are out of sight, gather up your energy and leap high off the ground in a different direction. This way, your scent will have stopped where you jumped, and you can run away with ease."

The fox was very pleased. "Great thinking, Owl, thank you," he said.

It wasn't long before the poor fox was being chased through the woods again. Remembering the advice that the owl had given him, he leaped high in the air away from the dogs, leaving them far behind and confused. "That owl really is smart," he said to himself.

But soon the unlucky fox had another problem. He returned to the tall oak tree and called out for the wise owl.

"What can I help you with today, Fox?" she asked kindly.

"Well, Owl, I always seem to walk into the dogs' traps. I am tired of being chased. Is there some way I can tell if there is danger ahead?"

The owl swivelled her head, deep in thought. She shuffled along the branch, closer to the fox. "It is quite simple really," she said with a soft coo. "The next time you are approaching the woods or somewhere dangerous, find a safe place to stand, then bark a few times and listen carefully. If there are any dogs in the area, they will surely bark in response. This will tell you that it is dangerous and that you must leave swiftly."

"Thank you, Owl," said the fox. Later that day he was looking for some food near the lake. He hid behind an old boat, barked three times, then listened. The fox jumped with fear when he heard two sharp growls in the distance. He darted off quickly, away from the danger. "That owl really is clever," he said to himself.

The next day the fox returned to the tall oak tree yet again. "Hello, Owl," he greeted.

"Yes, Fox?" said the owl in a somewhat tired voice.

"I am sorry to bother you again," said the fox, "but I have another problem and I don't know what to do. I am covered in fleas. I am terribly itchy. My coat is sore and raw. I can't get rid of them."

The Owl shook her feathers, deep in thought. "I have a plan," she said. "You must go to the lily pond nearby. Walk slowly into the water, until you are almost completely submerged. Leave your nose sticking out, of course, so you can breathe. The fleas will drown and your skin will feel soothed."

"Thank you, Owl," said the fox.

The fox did as he was told and was thrilled to be rid of the pesky fleas. His coat was clear and shiny. "That Owl really is marvellous," he said to himself.

A week later, the fox returned to the tall oak tree. "Are you there, Owl?" he called.

"Hello, Fox," replied the owl.

"Can you come closer, Owl? I can barely see you."

The owl shuffled along the branch, closer to the fox. "Can I help you with something?" she asked.

"Please come a bit closer, Owl. I can barely hear you."

The Owl shifted further along the branch, to the very edge.

"I wanted to thank you for your fantastic advice," said the fox. "You have helped me so very much. But there is one last thing I need your help with."

"What is that?" asked the owl suspiciously.

"I cut my foot while being chased," said the fox. "It is a very deep wound. Would you come down and examine it?"

The owl took one step back and said, "You arrived here with a spring in your step, and looked quite happy. Not the mood of one with an injured foot."

The fox became serious. "Are you calling me a liar?" he said in a threatening tone.

The owl took another step backwards. "No, of course not. Stretch out your foot, Fox. My eyesight is the best in the land, I can see perfectly well from up here.

The fox kept his foot hidden. "Forget it!" he snapped disrespectfully, and turned to leave.

"Oh, Fox, how sad you have made me," called the owl. "You think you can outsmart me, the wisest in the land? I helped you with all your troubles, and this is how you thank me. I will not come down off my tree to be your dinner. Shame on you!"

The fox blushed with embarrassment and ran from the tall oak tree. The wise owl is still perched in the same place, continuing to help those in need. However, those who are dishonest and ungrateful will not share in her knowledge.

The End

Bees in a Bottle

*T*om and Paul were best friends. During the summer holidays, the boys would spend almost every day together. They played hide and seek, swam in the lake, but most of all, they got up to mischief. They liked to play tricks on people, and were often cheeky. Most people agreed that they got away with things too lightly.

Tom and Paul got a job at a recycling centre for part of the summer. On their first day, the boys were shown around the property by the manager, Mr Samson. "You will be working outside," he said. The boys were shocked when they saw a mountain of bottles, stacked high in the air. Their job was to place different types of bottles into their correct crates. Then the bottles would be cleaned and transported to a factory for recycling. It was a very nice job indeed.

"It will take us forever to sort all these out!" said Tom.

"Don't be silly. Get down to work, and you will be finished by evening," said Mr Samson. The sun beat down, glistening off the glass bottles. There were large and small bottles, of all shapes and every colour, scattered about all over the place.

"Listen … Do you hear that?" said Paul. "Bzzz, bzzz."

The boys jumped back when they noticed a circle of bees hovering above their heads.

"Look over here!" cried Tom. There were bees everywhere. They were crawling in and out of the bottles, drinking up the last sticky drops left in them. "I have a wicked idea," said Paul. "Let's trap some bees in the bottles."

"Yeah, that'd be fun. Our little prisoners," laughed Tom.

The boys would wait until a bee walked into a bottle. Then they turned it upside down, balancing it on end and trapping the helpless insect inside. The little

creatures buzzed frantically within the sticky glass tubes. Bumping their noses time and time again, desperate to escape. The boys laughed at one bottle which had four confused bees buzzing inside.

Little did they realise that a bee is not something you want to trifle with. Soon they tired of trapping the bees and stopped to drink some water.

"What is going on here?" boomed a loud voice behind them. "You have not even started your work." It was Mr Samson.

He didn't notice the bees in their delicately balanced bottles, and knocked over some of them. Suddenly a choir of angry buzzing filled the air. An army of bees was circling Mr Samson and the boys. "Ouch!" "Aarrgghh!" "Yikes!" they all cried. The bees were not happy about being trapped. They stung Tom, Paul and poor Mr Samson over and over again. The boys jumped around in pain and panic, knocking over more of the bottles. Now all the bees were free. They stung Tom and Paul on the arms, on the legs and on the face. Red bumps quickly sprang up all over their bodies.

Mr Samson rushed the boys inside and slammed the door behind them. "You are the cruellest children I have ever met," he said furiously. "If you had just done your work, the bees would have left you alone, and you wouldn't have been stung."

It took two weeks for the boys to fully recover. Their mothers soaked the stings with vinegar. It hurt terribly with each drop, and smelled awful. The boys could barely sleep at night, as their whole bodies were sore from the bee stings. Their parents made them do all the house chores for being so cruel. They were woken up early every morning, and sent to bed early each night.

With two weeks of summer left, the boys asked Mr Samson for their jobs back at the recycling centre. They apologised for their foolishness and promised to work extra hard. They kept their word, and now the boys work in the centre

every summer. Tom and Paul learned a great lesson. Never be cruel to bees, or to any animals.

The End

Hooked

The sun beamed through the sky, glittering across the smooth surface of Caragh Lake. Rays of light cut through the dark water, illuminating the world underneath. There was a feeling of peace in the air, a true summer's day. A young trout named Finley swam slowly with his brother and sister beneath the surface.

Finley was feeling hungry. His eyes scanned constantly across the lake floor, watching for any sudden movements. He was not having much luck. He checked in with his siblings, but they too were finding it difficult to find lunch.

"I am going further up the lake," announced Finley.

His brother and sister exchanged a worried glance. "Mom and Dad said it is dangerous up there," said his sister.

Finley was always strongminded. "Don't worry about me," he replied.

He left his family behind and swam fast towards the north end of the lake. The water gradually became deeper and darker, and the sun-dappled lake floor faded into blackness. The pleasant warmth of the day turned to an icy chill. The plants here were no longer small and green; they were tall and wild. The fish were bigger too; one shot a menacing glance at Finley as he swam past.

Then Finley stopped in amazement. The juiciest, most delicious-looking worm he had ever seen was dangling in front of his eyes, suspended halfway between the lake floor and the water's surface. It wriggled from side to side, but did not swim away. Finley kept his wide eyes locked onto the worm as he slowly and smoothly glided towards it. Surely this was too good to be true – such a delicious lunch, just waiting for him. He glanced around, but no, there were no other fish nearby. It was all his.

Finley opened his mouth as wide as he could and snapped down hard. A sharp sting of pain seared into the top of his mouth. The water started to stain with drops of red. Poor Finley had no idea what had just happened. He had never

heard of a stinging worm before. He tried to spit it out, but he couldn't, and the pain grew worse. Something hard and metal was firmly stuck in his jaw.

Finley turned to swim for home, but when he moved there was a sharp tug in his mouth and he was whirled back to where he started. The tugging continued and he could feel himself being dragged upwards. The sunlight was dazzling as he was pulled near the lake's surface. Finley thrashed and twisted, but it was no use; the more he fought, the faster he rose. Finley's heart was pounding fast. He now knew that the worm was attached to a fisherman's hook.

The little fish was tugged up out of the water. Finley gasped, startled by the bright sun. It was difficult to catch his breath.

"We got one, we got one!" the fishermen shouted. Finley felt hopeless. The men were strong and there was no way to escape. Tears fell from the little fish's eyes and rippled in the lake below.

"Reel him in, quick!" he heard one man say. Finley swayed back and forth on the line as the fisherman steadily moved his hand at the base of the fishing rod. Through the corner of his eye, Finley saw something jumping towards the boat. It was his brother and sister! Finley was filled with hope and courage at this sight. He was almost within the fishermen's grasp when he put up an almighty fight.

Using all his strength, Finley kicked his tail up and down and from side to side. He swung away from the fisherman. "Hold on tight," said one of the men. Finley could feel the hook in his mouth loosen with each thrash of his tail. He kicked and kicked, until finally he felt the pressure cease in his mouth. Finley plummeted down through the air. The boat and the men's faces drifted further and further away. He hit the lake's surface with a smack and sank into the deep blue water. His dry body welcomed the cool liquid. Finley quickly swam deeper into the lake, fearing that he would be caught again.

He heard his name being called out. It was his brother and sister. After a few happy tears, they swam together back to the shallow part of the lake.

"I warned you not to venture up there," said his sister. "I will be highly suspicious of any worm I ever see again," he replied, exhausted.

It was the first and last encounter Finley ever had with a fisherman. He had learned a frightening lesson. From that day onwards, he warned every fish he met of the dangers of an easy meal.

The End

Graffiti

When I was a young boy, I went to stay with my grandmother every summer. She lives in a small seaside town. It is a beautiful place, and I spend a lot of my time there painting pictures of it – the sea, the trees, the old castle on its craggy rocks.

People in the town knew that I loved to paint. I could often be spotted sitting on a rock, or high up in the trees, trying to capture the rugged landscape. I spent hours concentrating on the crashing waves and golden sand. Then I would rush back to my grandmother's house, and proudly show her my latest creation.

One quiet evening, my grandmother sent me to buy some milk. It was almost six o'clock and the shop was about to close. I took some money and rushed out the door. Just a few yards before the store, I noticed a group of boys standing in front of the large wall that separates the road from the beach. They were painting something on the wall with spray cans. "There's someone here!" hissed one of the boys in panic. Their heads shot around and looked at me with terror. Then they dropped the cans and ran off.

I approached the wall. It was dripping with black and red paint. It was obvious that this was done without permission, and it looked awful. I picked up the dripping spray cans and threw them in the rubbish bin beside the shop. Then I went in and bought the milk that I had set out for.

When I got back, my grandmother was pacing back and forth, with a troubled look on her face. "Is everything okay, Nan?" I asked.

She turned her piercing eyes on me. "No, Ethan, everything is not okay. Something terrible has happened. The old stone wall near Murphy's shop was vandalised. It is smeared in ugly red and black paint," she said. "It happened earlier this evening. And to make it worse, someone has telephoned and said that you are responsible."

I sat down in shock. "Mrs Murphy in the shop said that you came in to buy the

milk, and that your jumper was stained with red and black paint," said my grandmother.

"But it wasn't me, Nan," I said quickly. "I arrived at the scene of the crime. The boys ran away when they saw me. I dumped the spray cans in the bin, and I must have got some paint on my jumper."

My grandmother looked relieved. "We will have to go to the police and explain everything this minute," she said.

On our way through the town, I heard people whispering about the spray cans. Men and women pointed at me with angry stares. They knew that I loved to paint, but I couldn't do anything like that! I felt terrible.

The police were a little bit scary. They asked me questions until I was exhausted. I did my best to describe the three boys. They kept asking about the paint on my clothes, even though I explained about dumping the cans.

The next few days were very tough. I stayed inside, not even going out to paint. My grandmother tried to cheer me up, but I was too down. I went to bed early each night.

On Friday, just as we were sitting down to lunch, there was a knock at the door. "Who could that be?" I wondered. There, standing in the doorway, were a policeman and a member of the Town Council.

"Hello young man, are you Ethan?" they asked. "We have come to apologise to you. You have been through a difficult few days. We have caught the boys who vandalised the wall, and they are going to be punished."

My grandmother hugged me tight. "Thank goodness," she said.

The Town Council man looked at me. "I hear that you are a very good artist," he said. "The people of the town were wondering if you would consider doing a painting over the mess on the wall?"

I didn't hesitate. "I would love to!" I told him.

Later that same day, I went to look at the wall. There were two boys waiting for

me, each carrying a big box full of tins of paint, in every colour imaginable. "What are you going to paint?" they asked, wide-eyed.

"The old castle on the rock, with the ocean on the horizon," I said with excitement. I had never done such a big painting before.

When it was finally finished, two weeks later, all the people of the town came and marvelled at the new artwork. "Isn't it lovely?" said a couple. "Oh, it's gorgeous," said Mrs Murphy, the shopkeeper. The local newspaper had sent a reporter to take my picture beside the wall. What had started out as a terrible summer had turned into the best summer ever!

The End

Home at Last

hayla the spider had been walking for a very long time. Her eight legs were frightfully tired. She could see a large house in the distance. "I will be safe in there," she thought. Shayla reached the house, scaled the wall and climbed up onto a window ledge. The window was slightly open, so she crawled inside, landing on the floor with a thud.

The unnatural light inside the house was dazzling. Shayla quickly scampered across the floor, and slipped under a bed. It was dark and dusty, which she liked. Just as she was about to go for a nap, she heard a loud scraping sound. Someone was brushing the floor. Shayla hid in the corner and hoped she would be safe. The broom poked and prodded under the bed. "I have to get out of here," she panicked.

The spider made a dash from under the bed. "Eeeekk!" cried the woman who was sweeping. Shayla ran as fast as she could, never once looking back. She soon found herself in the living room. She crawled along the fluffy carpet, stopping now and then to catch her breath. Then she saw a man towering above her, holding a rolled-up newspaper. He suddenly smashed the paper down to the ground, almost hitting her.

Shayla rushed along the floor and crept under the television set. She could hear people talking. "There is a horrible spider under the TV. Ughhhh, I hate spiders," they said.

Shayla felt so alone. "If only I could meet some other spiders," she thought sadly. "Then I would be happy." Late that night, when everyone was sleeping, Shayla left the shelter of the television in search of some food. Spiders can see very well in the dark, so she had no trouble getting around. She squeezed through the gap under a door, and entered the bathroom.

Shayla climbed up the side of the bathtub and slid all the way down into the bath. That was fun! Shayla had no idea what a bath was. A human house was a whole new world to her. The little spider drank some water from the drain. Then she

tried to climb back up out of the bath. It was impossible. Again and again, she almost made it to the top, then lost her footing and tumbled back down. "Oh dear," she sobbed.

The next morning, a little boy was washing his hands in the sink. "Huuhh?" he gasped. "What do we have here?" Shayla stayed perfectly still. The little boy cupped his hands together and scooped up the spider. "Put me down! Put me down!" Shayla shrieked. The little boy brought the spider to his parents. "Oh my!" cried his mother. "Put that thing outside at once."

The little boy went out to the garden, and carefully placed the spider on the ground. At first, Shayla was excited to be out of the house and away from danger. But she still didn't know where she was, and the garden was full of all sorts of insects, birds and animals.

She combed through the grassy jungle and came out onto a pathway. Now she saw another building. It was some sort of shed, much smaller than the house. She marched on towards it and peeked inside. Shayla felt safer in this building. There were lots of old boxes, logs and paint tins scattered around. She crept under an old chair and had a little rest.

"Hello there," said a soft voice. Shayla looked around and saw a little brown spider, sitting on a log. "What's your name?" he asked.

"I'm Shayla, and I am looking for a place to stay," she answered shyly.

"Well, you are in luck! There are all sorts of spiders here. My name is Spike," he added with a friendly grin. "Where did you come from?"

"I was lost," said Shayla with a shiver, "and then I came across a big house. I went inside, but I was chased everywhere. I certainly wasn't welcome there. It seems that people don't really like spiders. I didn't mean any harm," she explained sadly.

Spike nodded his head in sympathy. "It's true, people don't understand spiders. They can be very mean. Anyway, you are safe here now. You had better start spinning your web if you want a comfortable place to sleep tonight."

Shayla found the perfect place for her web, in a lovely dark corner of the shed. She climbed up the wall and quickly started spinning silk threads. An hour later, she had crafted a beautiful orb web. All the other spiders came out to marvel at her beautiful creation.

"You are very talented" said an old spider with grey spots.

"Will you help me with my web?" asked a tiny black spider.

Shayla had found the home she was looking for. She quickly made friends with all of the other spiders, and was admired greatly for her talent at spinning beautiful webs. There was lots of good food to be found, and plenty of dark, dusty corners to explore. Shayla slept well amongst the other spiders in the garden shed.

The End

A Trip to Kerry

Sisters Amy and Jessie Sullivan arrived in County Kerry, in the very southwest corner of Ireland. It was great to be away from the busy city of Dublin and enjoying the freedom of the open countryside. Peaceful sounds and beautiful scenes surrounded them. It had been a very long drive, but it would be worth it, their parents told them.

The first stop of the day, not far from their hotel in Killarney, was the Kerry Bog Village. "This is an old famine town, from the early nineteenth century, with five thatched cottages," said Mr Sullivan.

The girls peered into one dark and smoky cottage. "This house must have been only for one person," announced Jessie.

"Oh no," said her mother, "sometimes families of ten or more people lived in these cottages."

Jessie looked appalled. "But where did they all sleep?"

Her mother laughed and replied, "On the floor, on roll-out mattresses, and as many squeezed into the one bed as possible."

The girls noticed that some of the houses were larger than others, so some families were a little more comfortable than others. Overall, though, life was difficult during this time for everyone. People had little food and worked hard all day long.

Seeing how people had lived long ago made the girls a little bit sad, but they also felt grateful that times had changed – life was much easier today. "Let's go and see the animals now," suggested Amy.

There were two enormous dogs in an enclosed area. "They are Irish wolfhounds," said their father.

"They are huge!" chimed the girls.

"Irish wolfhounds are the largest dogs in the world," said their father. "They were once used for hunting wolves. But wolves no longer exist in Ireland, they are all gone now."

"What happened to them?" asked the girls.

"They became a nuisance as more and more people lived here. They were dangerous, so the people hunted them all down and wiped them out. Irish wolfhounds played a big part in that."

Jessie stroked one of the hounds. He panted loudly, with his big sloppy tongue hanging out. He looked very content. His golden-brown eyes darted from left to right, taking in all the smiling faces admiring him. He looked so friendly and charming that the girls found it hard to imagine him fighting a ferocious wolf. "They also fought brown bears and wild elk, which also roamed Ireland at one time. Wolfhounds have seen many animals come and go. They do look friendly, but appearances can be deceiving," laughed the girls' mother.

The girls left the dogs and strolled over to some small, strong-looking ponies. "These are Kerry Bog Ponies, native to Kerry," said a man standing nearby. "They were used for transport one hundred years ago. They would carry turf from the bogs, and seaweed from the beach."

One of the ponies approached the two girls, looking at them with beautiful, dark eyes. He was eleven hands high and hazelnut brown in colour, with a long, flaxen mane. Jessie stroked the little star in the middle of his forehead. "Good boy," she said affectionately.

When they had finished looking around the village, the Sullivan family got back into their car and set off again. "Where are we going now, Mom?" asked Jessie. "You are in for a great treat, girls," said their mother. "We are going to Skellig Michael."

The car pulled in at the side of a cliff. The family got out, startled by the strong wind. The Atlantic Ocean sprawled out in front of them, heaving up and down in a hypnotic way.

"What is that big rock out in the distance?" asked Amy. It was black and jagged looking, sticking straight up out of the sea.

"I'm glad you asked," smiled her father. "That is Skellig Michael. It is an extremely old and historical place. People lived there way back in the sixth century.

Amy looked appalled again. "People lived out there?" she repeated with a gulp.

"Oh yes, important people for that matter. They were monks. They liked to live in isolation, far from other people. They created beautiful, brightly coloured books, called scriptures, painting with pens made from goose feathers. Come on, let's go there and see for ourselves."

The family drove to the harbour and boarded a beautiful white boat. There were lots of other excited tourists on deck. The engine revved and the boat took off speedily, bouncing over the waves. Amy and Jessie's hair blew in the wind, and a fine spray of water splashed over the people sitting at the back.

The water was choppy and uneven, making the journey fun for the girls, but terrible for their father who suffered from sea sickness.

"Look at all the birds!" said their mother. Gannets, puffins and sea gulls were flying though the air, squawking noisily. "There is a gannet bird colony near here. It is known as Little Michael, as it is smaller than Skellig Michael. It is the second biggest gannet colony in the world, after Bonaventure Island in Canada."

The girls gasped as they got closer to Skellig Michael. The huge rocky island loomed over them, dark and dangerous-looking. The water was pitch dark around the island, the sunlight blocked out by the steep rocks.

Amy and Jessie were first out of the boat, closely followed by their parents.

It felt amazing to be so isolated, standing on a rock way out in the Atlantic Ocean. "Incredible!" said Amy.

"Let's see if you still like it in a few hours. We have to climb to the top now," said their mother.

Six hundred and forty deep steps wrapped around the island, climbing all the way to the summit. The girls started running over as many steps as they could, but they soon had to sit and catch their breath. "Better to go at a steady pace all the way," warned their father.

When they climbed onto the last step, the Sullivan family were tired. Before they had a chance to rest, though, a man appeared with a walking stick. "Follow me, everyone," he said in a husky voice.

Just around the corner lay a ruined settlement. There were funny-looking dome-shaped houses, called beehive huts. "They look just like igloos," suggested Jessie.

There was also a church and two drinking wells, enclosed by a long stone wall.

"Saint Fionán founded this monastic settlement in the sixth century, and monks lived here until the thirteenth century," the man informed them.

"Was it difficult to live here?" asked the girls' father.

"Yes indeed. There are often great storms here in the middle of the sea. However, the monks lived a very simple life here. They would go fishing for their food, grow vegetables and pray in the church. The huts are round on the outside, but rectangular on the inside. They were built in a special way, so that no rain could get in. This place is so old and special that it is protected by UNESCO and is on the world's heritage list.

"It is amazing to know that people have been on this island centuries before us," thought the girls.

After lots of photographs and a much needed picnic, the Sullivan family returned to the boat. Far too soon, they were in their car, driving back to the city. "Kerry truly is a magical and mystical place," said the girls.

The End

The Wild Horse

The rain showered down from the black night sky. Thunder boomed angrily and bursts of lightning startled me. My father and I were finishing our day's work, feeding the animals on the farm. My brothers were sweeping and cleaning around the yard. The rain fell so hard I could barely keep my eyes open.

My brother suddenly called out for my father. His voice was full of urgency, and we all ran to him. We were stunned at what we saw. It was the most beautiful horse we had ever set eyes on, saturated from the rain and panting loudly. She was bay coloured, tall and elegant, with a small white star in the middle of her face.

"Hush, hush," my father said, slowly approaching her with his hand reached out. Every step my father took was met with a step backwards by the horse. She quietened her breathing, but her eyes were wild and untrusting. My father stopped. "Get some hay and water," he said to my brother, not taking his eyes off her.

She pawed her front leg on the ground a few times, with a piercing sound that only a frightened horse can make. We edged backwards nervously. Then she reared up onto her hind legs, towering over us like a threatening giant. My little brother fell over a tin bucket and landed flat on his back. The bucket clattered noisily on the stone yard. The horse turned abruptly and struck out with her hind legs. My father shielded us. "Go away, shoo, shoo!" he shouted at her. She galloped away at great speed into the darkness. The ground vibrated under the pounding of her hooves.

I helped my sobbing brother off the ground. We went inside the house to my mother. "You are very lucky you didn't get hurt," she said, with a worried look. That night I went to bed and had a vivid dream about the horse. It was a sunny day and she was alone in a beautiful meadow. Now she wasn't angry or scared. She walked slowly and confidently. I walked up to her and patted her face. Her eyes were soft and kind.

I told my father about the dream. "That's a dream all right," he laughed. "That animal is wild and dangerous. If she comes near here again there's no telling what I might do."

Later I went outside to get some logs for the fire. There was a full moon in the sky, and it was dry and calm. I threw each heavy log into the basket, one by one. Then the hairs stood up on the back of my neck. I knew I was being watched. I turned around, and there she was – the same horse, looking straight at me. At first I felt afraid. But this time the horse didn't look frightened. She took a few steps forward. I stayed very still, allowing her to be in control. She nudged her head against my arm and sniffed at my shoulder, her nostrils flaring loudly. I reached out and patted her neck.

She had marks on her body from mistreatment. Perhaps she has run away, I thought. I heard a door open behind me. "James!" my mother called. The horse turned around so fast she knocked over the basket of logs I was gathering. My mother saw the horse and screamed for my father. "It's alright," I assured them. They looked at the fallen logs and assumed I had been attacked. I told them about the marks across the horse's shoulders and barrel. "She must have been beaten away in defence," they decided.

When a week had passed and the horse had not returned, I grew worried. I knew she had only been confused and frightened on that rainy night. I knew she was a gentle animal that had been mistreated. Where could she be?

One day, my father and I were moving a herd of sheep to another paddock, further up the mountain. It was a tricky task, as the sheep were unruly and kept scattering in all directions. My father yelled at me every time the sheep did not move where he wanted them.

As we moved higher up the mountain, the ground got more rugged and it was more difficult to keep the sheep together. They had split into different groups, and one bunch was not moving at all. I was sweating and out of breath. Then I heard something behind me. I turned, and saw a horse galloping towards us. She trotted right up next to me.

"Go back, Go back!" my father shouted in panic. The horse looked at me and shook her head from side to side. I reached out and stroked her cheek. She turned and ran away. We watched in amazement as she circled the sheep. The sheep closed into a single, tight group. She ran back to me, a proud look in her eyes. "Let's go," I said to my dad.

My father watched, amazed, as the horse skillfully kept the sheep at a steady pace. Every time they went off track, she picked up speed and cornered them off. We soon got to the new paddock, and my father locked the gate behind the flock.

We walked back to the farm and I led the horse into a stable. "You were right, son. She has welts on her body. Whoever owned her was cruel and negligent. Well, she is safe now in her new home, here with us," said my father with a smile.

My father and I grew very close to the horse. We named her Star Light, because of the little star on her forehead and because she appeared like a bright star into our lives on that rainy night.

She helped us move the sheep every week, and I soon learned to ride. I still have her today, and we spend many days trotting along the beach and through the countryside. She is my closest companion.

My Fly Away Kite

Kaydn's favourite toy in the world was his kite. He lived right next to the beach, where there were strong winds, great for flying. He would run along the sand, watching as the invisible force of the wind lifted his kite higher and higher. He was very skilled at controlling the kite, and his friends and family would look on in amazement as Kaydn made it twirl and dance.

One very windy day, Kaydn went onto the strand to try out his new kite. It was a gift from his cousin. He knew it was expensive, as it was much larger than his other kite and it was made from a very fine cloth. It was shaped and painted like an eagle. Kaydn was very excited. He couldn't wait to see it fly for the first time.

Kaydn gripped the handle tightly, and let the kite free. The line quickly unwound and the eagle kite soared up into the sky. It swooped and swirled, high above his head. Kaydn ran along the beach, making sure it never dropped too low. It looked like a real eagle, hovering in the air.

Kaydn was concentrating so hard on the kite that he did not notice a large sandcastle up ahead. He ran straight into it, tripped over and crashed face-first into the mushy wet sand. Sitting up, he spat sand from his mouth and rubbed it from his stinging eyes. Kaydn jumped to his feet when he realised he had let go of his new kite.

He looked to the sky. "Oh No!" he whimpered. It had blown up against the cliffs, and was tangled on a little, stunted tree. How would he ever get it back? His mind was racing and his heart was beating fast. "Maybe if I am careful I can climb up and get it," he thought foolishly.

The little boy started to climb the tall cliff face. The rocks were wet and muddy, and full of loose stones. Kaydn scratched his hand against a protruding rock. "Ouch!" he winced. Then it started to rain. This made climbing even more difficult, and his footing more unstable. He didn't dare to look down, in case he lost his nerve. But Kaydn was determined to retrieve his kite. He foolishly

ignored the danger and continued to scale the steep cliff.

Eventually, sore and wet and splattered with mud, Kaydn reached the eagle kite. He turned around for the first time, and got a bad fright. It was a very long way down. There was no way he could climb back to the beach without slipping. "I will have to stay here until it stops raining," he decided.

An hour passed, and the rain continued to pour down. Kaydn was getting dizzy watching the powerful waves crashing against the rocks, way down below. He was beginning to regret his actions. "I should have just gone home," he sobbed.

Kaydn held on tighter to the jagged rock as the wind rose. He was shivering with the cold. It was still raining and his clothes were soaked through. Then he saw two figures far off in the distance. "Help! Help!" he roared. They started to run towards him. It was his school friend Jill, and her father, Mr Philips. "I am coming to get you. Hold on," Mr Philips shouted.

He was tall and strong, and a skilled climber. He moved steadily up the cliff face until he reached Kaydn. "Give me your hand," he called out. Kaydn held his kite under one arm and reached out for Mr Philips with the other. Slowly they edged down the cliff together, until they were safely on the ground.

"What on earth were you doing up there?" asked Jill angrily.

"I was trying to get my kite. It got stuck on the cliff," he replied sheepishly.

"You could have been hurt, or worse!" said Mr Philips sternly.

When Kaydn got home, his parents were fuming with anger. "How could you be so reckless? You risked your life and health for a toy!" they yelled. Kaydn was sent upstairs to his room. He sat on his bed and examined his new kite. It was broken. There were two large rips at the back of the eagle's wings. "What a dreadful day this is," he muttered. Kaydn cried himself to sleep that night.

Although Kaydn had broken his new kite, he had also learned a valuable lesson. Toys and gifts are wonderful, but they are not as important as being safe. If a

situation is dangerous, you must seek help from others. Kaydn still flies kites. He loves to watch them soaring up into the sky, but he is happy to stay on the ground.

The End

Fungi the Dolphin

My name is Fungi. I am a bottle-nosed dolphin. I live in the waters off Dingle in County Kerry, Ireland. Most days I scour the bay for small fish to eat, or I race with my fellow dolphins. People say that I am special. Why am I not afraid of people, like the other dolphins? Well, let me tell you.

One cloudy morning, many years ago, I was swimming in Dingle Bay when I noticed a curious shadow above me. I peered up through the water and saw a man in a boat. At first he did not see me. I swam underneath the boat for a while, wondering what he was doing. He was singing a little song to himself, and looked friendly.

I dipped down deep under the water. Then I turned and swam to the surface as fast as I could, bursting out of the water and high into the air. The man looked amazed and smiled broadly. I slapped back down into the ocean and swam beside his boat. Each time I jumped out of the sea, he laughed and clapped with enthusiasm. It was a great feeling.

I told the other dolphins of my experience. They were horrified.

"People are dangerous creatures. You should stay clear of them," they warned.

But I was looking forward to meeting a person again. I began swimming in close to the shore, watching the docked boats and passers-by.

A few days later, I saw another shadow on top of the water. This one was large, and moving fast. I swam up to the surface and saw that there were many people on this boat, chatting and taking pictures. I let my dorsal fin break the surface and kept alongside the boat. "A shark, a shark!" I heard a little boy cry.

"That's not a shark, it is a dolphin," corrected his mother.

Once again I dipped low, then swam up and shot high out of the water. I could hear the people gasp and clap. This really was fun! Then I noticed the same

little boy leaning out dangerously over the edge of the boat. He didn't have a lifejacket on. Suddenly I felt very uneasy.

I squeaked and clicked warnings to the people on the boat, but they couldn't understand me. The little boy let out a frightened wail as he toppled over the railing. He splashed hard into the dark, choppy water.

At first I felt afraid of the boy. I had never come so close to a human before. "Help! Help!" he shrieked. His face was turning white from the cold and he looked terribly frightened. He kept disappearing under the water. I had to do something.

The people on the boat were frantic and screaming.

"We're coming, we're coming," they yelled.

I swam cautiously toward the boy. He lurched towards me and grabbed onto my dorsal fin. He held on tightly, gasping for air. I stayed perfectly still, anchoring him. The boat was turning to get back to us.

The little boy looked straight into my eyes. "Thank you," he whispered.

A tall man threw down an orange float. Then the boy let go of me and clasped onto the life ring. Two men started to hoist the boy upwards. "Thank heavens!" his mother said, pale and teary-eyed. Everyone started clapping joyfully, hugging each other and taking photographs.

The people waved at me. "He saved my life, Mom," said the boy in a shaky voice.

"Yes, he did," his mother replied, hugging him fiercely. I jumped up from the water again and again, leading the boat back to shore.

Word travelled fast about me saving the little boy. Now, boatloads of people from all over the world come out into the harbour every week, especially to see me. I enjoy putting on a show and receiving applause. In the evenings I return to my

dolphin friends. They are still shy of people, and to be honest, are a little bit jealous of all the fun that I have.

The End

The Lucky Swan

One day after school, Hunter the swan told his parents that he was going up to Mason's Creek.

"Who are you going with?" they asked.

"Oh, just myself. Don't worry, I will be back for dinner at six," he replied, already bustling out through the reeds.

Mason's Creek is a very quiet place, covered in rushes and overhanging trees. Swans rarely go there, as the water is murky and shallow, but Hunter loved exploring and adventure. He didn't have many friends, and loved to just go off by himself, finding new places and seeing new sights.

It was a peaceful swim across Layton Lake. Hunter glided slowly over the water, admiring the majestic surroundings. Huge alder trees framed the lake, and tall mountains were reflected on its smooth surface. It was a quiet evening, and there were few birds in the sky. "Hello!" shouted the swan. He heard his voice echo around him again and again.

Hunter waddled up out of the lake, shaking his feathers dry. He was making his way into a wooded area, when a strange feeling came over him, like he was being watched. He turned around sharply, but there was nothing there. As he walked on, he heard a low grumbling sound. "Gggrrrrrrrrrr." Hunter turned again, and this time he saw a glowing pair of eyes amongst the bushes.

Hunter forced himself to remain calm. He edged slowly backwards into the woods, keeping his eyes fixed on the shadowy creature. It was following him. Hunter held his breath and felt his skin prickling. "Stay back," he hissed. The creature let out a terrifying roar as it stepped out into the open. Hunter's heart skipped a beat. It was a wolf! Long and muscular, with a huge mouth full of razor-sharp teeth, it had a deadly look in its eyes. A dangerous grin spread across its face as it watched Hunter closely.

Hunter couldn't fly away. There wasn't enough space between the trees to spread

his wings. He didn't have time to turn and run, as the wolf was ready to pounce. He felt his leg sinking. "Oh no," he panicked. He tried to pull it out, but it sank even faster. He was completely stuck. Looking down, he realised he had backed into a muddy swamp. The wolf spotted the swan's foot and licked its lips.

"Help, Help!" shouted the helpless swan. The wolf lowered its head and crept closer, but stopped at the swamp's edge. It didn't want to get stuck as well.

Hunter snapped and hissed furiously at the wolf. He had never felt such fear. The wolf stretched its long snout out towards the swan, sniffing at its neck. Feathers flew through the air as Hunter flapped his wings as hard as he could. The wolf was not fazed by this. It just laughed menacingly at the helpless bird.

The wolf snarled, showing a huge set of jagged dagger-shaped teeth. Hunter felt dizzy and weak. Then there was a loud howl behind him. Hunter turned his head, only to see another, even bigger, wolf. Hunter snapped his beak at the second wolf. He knew he could not win – a helpless swan, stuck in a swamp, against two savage wolves. "This is the end of me" he sobbed to himself.

The second wolf prowled closer and closer. He licked his lips and drooled horribly. Hunter closed his eyes and feared the worst. But nothing happened.

He opened his eyes. The two wolves were now glaring at each other in rage. This was Hunter's chance. He flapped his wings with all his might, and felt his leg lifting up out of the mud. The wolves never once looked his way; their eyes were fixed on each other. With the last of his strength, Hunter lifted out of the swamp, landing head-first in the bushes. Just at that moment, the first wolf launched itself into the air, tackling the other wolf to the ground.

They wrestled fiercely, roaring with fury. A hurricane of teeth and blood flashed before Hunter's eyes. Hunter knew that he had only moments to escape. He turned his back on the wolves and dashed towards the lake, flapping his wings. Just when he thought he was safe, he felt a painful clamp down on his foot, he had been bit. He torpedoed straight down into the water. He swam frantically until he was at the deepest part of the lake, then he turned around to look. The

two wolves were standing hungrily at the water's edge, wounded and defeated.

Hunter returned home, and told his family and friends about the dangers of Mason's Creek. He admitted it was very foolish to travel by himself, especially to unknown areas. Everyone agreed that he was extremely lucky to have lived to tell the tale.

The End

Iced Milk

There once lived a horrible Irish Wolfhound named Fion. He towered above the other animals, and his menacing gaze could make a smaller animal freeze in terror. His grey, scruffy coat was matted and smelly. Time and time again, other animals reached out to be his friend, but it was no use.

Fion loved barking and growling. This always gave the other animals a terrible scare. "Woof, woof, woof!" he barked, all day long. Birds would fly away in fear, and the terrible racket made the cats' ears sting.

One day, Fion did something extra terrible. He chased Cassie the Cat away from her home, where she had lived all her life. He hunted her over hills, around trees and through hedges, until she was completely lost. Days passed and she did not return. Kendall the Kitten and Larry the Labrador decided that they would have to teach Fion a lesson.

"We must show Fion that we won't accept this behaviour," said Larry. "We are all exhausted from running around all day, and his constant barking is too much to bear. He must be taught some manners."

"But what can we do? He is so big!" whimpered Kendall.

The weather was getting very cold. It had snowed for the last few days. "Hmmm," said Larry thoughtfully. "Fion gets his food at four o'clock. His owners always leave him some meat and a bowl of milk, just outside the door."

"We could take his food?" said Kendall. "That would teach him a lesson."

"No, no, he would know who did it straight away. He would smell the trail with his big nose," dismissed Larry.

"I have a marvellous idea," said one of the birds. "How about we get his empty bowl, before he is fed. We could fill it with water, and put some snow in too. It will freeze over, and look just like a bowl of milk. If he drinks it, his tongue will get stuck. It will be hilarious," she chirped.

"Great idea," the animals agreed.

They hid in the bushes in the garden and waited until Fion was fast asleep. Even when sleeping, Fion was noisy; his snoring could be heard from the end of the garden. Kendall crept towards the bowl, her light paws not making a sound. "It's empty," she whispered back to the others.

Larry picked up the bowl in his mouth and brought it over to the garden hose. He turned the nozzle and half-filled it with water. He pushed some snow in too, then carefully returned the bowl beside the sleeping wolfhound.

"Okay, let's go and watch from the bushes," they said. The lady of the house soon came out and placed some chicken and leftovers near Fion. Then she noticed the bowl of ice. "Oh, you didn't drink your milk, Fion," she said with surprise. The large dog opened his eyes when he smelled the food. "Woo, woof, woof!" he barked at the woman. "Oh, be quiet, you ungrateful mutt," she huffed.

The animals watched with excitement as Fion hungrily wolfed down his food. He licked his lips when he was finished. Now he was thirsty. Fion stood over the bowl of ice. It was creamy white and looked exactly like milk. He lowered his head to the bowl, and pressed his big, sloppy tongue right down against the ice.

"Arrrrgghhh!" he yelped. He was stuck. He lifted his head, but the bowl rose off the ground too and stayed firmly attached to his tongue. He shrieked at the terrible freezing pain in his mouth.

This is when all the animals emerged from the bushes. "Ha ha, ha ha," they all laughed.

"The joke is on you for a change," said Larry. Fion looked afraid and cowered into the corner. "We are teaching you some manners," said Kendall sadly. "You terrified Cassie the Cat. She is still missing." Fion scampered off, with the bowl trailing after him. It certainly was a funny sight to see.

The next day the animals were delighted to see Cassie the Cat return home. "You're back, you're back!" they cheered.

"Yes, and you will never believe what happened," she told them. "Fion found me. I thought he was going to chase me, but instead he apologised and led me

back here. He told me about the trick you played on him. His tongue is still sore," she giggled.

The animals forgave Fion and invited him to play their games with them. He accepted, and now he enjoys being part of the group, instead of scaring everyone.

The End

The Christmas Robin

One freezing cold Christmas night, my mother and I were gazing out the window, watching the snow drifting to the ground. My father and sister were chatting by the fire.

We thought of all the little animals in their burrows and nests, and in the bushes. How cold they must be! While we were speaking, a little robin redbreast appeared at our window. He was the cutest little thing, with tiny, sparkly eyes and a little beak that chirped and smiled at us. There were two green dots over his right eye. I opened the window slightly, and he immediately jumped up and perched on the frame. "Hello, little one," my mother said. "Tweet tweet" he chirped in reply.

"Come quick, look at this!" I called out to my father and sister. They laughed when they saw the little robin dancing along our window. "You must be freezing," said my sister Jane. "Tweet tweet," he replied. My mother went into the kitchen to get some blueberries. When she returned, the little robin hopped off the window and onto her hand. It was amazing to see a wild animal so friendly. He gobbled down all the berries, like they were the first bits of food he had eaten in ages. I got my camera and snapped some pictures.

When he had finished eating, my mother perched the little robin back outside. She stroked his little head and blew him a goodnight kiss.

The next morning, I woke up and ran to the living room, hoping the robin would still be at our window. But he was nowhere to be seen. The snow had melted too. I looked at the pictures in my camera and smiled.

A year passed, and it was Christmas again. The snow was falling heavily outside. My mother was cooking a delicious feast and my father was collecting turf for the fire. I went to the living room to search for a book. To my surprise, I spotted a little bird perched on our window frame, chirping loudly. As I came closer, I noticed the two little green dots over his right eye. When I opened the window, he jumped on my finger and I stroked his tiny chest.

"Mom," I called.

She ran into the room, and beamed a grin when she saw the same little robin. "We are going to have to give you a name," she said.

"How about Reddie?" suggested my sister, Jane.

"I like that," said my mother. "Reddie the Robbin".

Once again we gave the little robin food. We left the window open slightly, so he could hear us and wouldn't feel lonely. We really hoped he would still be there the next day. But, just like the year before, in the morning he had vanished. "Maybe we should build a little house for Reddie?" I said to my father. "That way he might stay with us next year."

"That's a great idea," he said cheerily.

Over the next few days, my father and I built a beautiful birdhouse. We used Pecan wood which we painted a glossy red. We placed a little basket inside the house to hold food.

Another year passed. It was Christmas morning again, and I jumped from my bed, bursting with excitement. I ran to the living room and looked through the window. Reddie was there! He looked terribly cold. He looked older and a little more fragile.

However, this year he was not alone. There was another little robin beside him. "Reddie has a friend – it's Mrs Reddie," laughed Jane.

Reddie flew up onto my shoulder. He chirped excitedly and flapped his wings. I scooped up the other robin, and carried them both to the birdhouse we had built. My mother appeared with lots of blueberries, which she placed in the little basket inside. We watched, delighted, as the two little birds ate the food and bounced up and down with joy. That night, I went to bed with a smile. Reddie had loved his Christmas gift.

The next morning, I woke late. I went to the kitchen for some breakfast. "Good morning, Davey," my mother smiled. "Did you have a look in the garden this

morning?" I put on my coat and boots, and ran out to see if Reddie was there. I couldn't see him anywhere in the garden. Then I quietly peered into the birdhouse, and saw two little heads snuggled together. Reddie woke up and popped outside. He chirped joyfully and I gently stroked his feathers. It was the first year that Reddie had stayed after Christmas day.

The two Robins flew back and forth from the nest. They gathered twigs and moss, and made the birdhouse truly their own. Soon after, there were baby robins. I was thrilled that Reddie had settled in our garden. For it is not many people who can say that they have a pet robin redbreast.

The End

Jerry Mulvihill was born on 7 December 1985, and raised in Ballintcleave, County Kerry, Ireland. He has a degree in Interior Design from Salford University, and also has a diploma in Journalism. Jerry enjoys painting, and in his spare time produces art and visits exhibitions. He started off writing poetry. His works have been recited on national radio, with one published in the book *Breaking the Silence* in 2003.

His debut book *Let's Read a Story*, published in summer 2011, received critical acclaim from Irish media, including RTÉ's Miriam O'Callaghan. This work was soon translated into French, selling out its first print run within a few months. Jerry released *The Wise Owl Storybook* in summer 2012. It will be available in German by the end of the year.

If you liked

The
Wise Owl
Storybook

be sure to check out my debut book

Let's Read a Story

Available in English and French

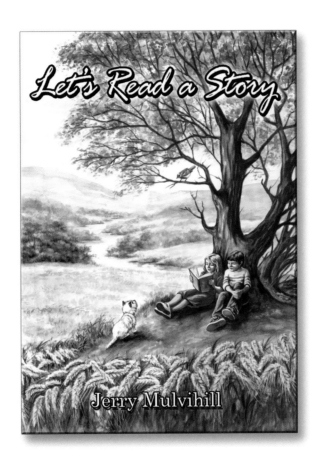

"A wonderful book!" Miriam O'Callaghan, RTÉ

"Kids will love it" The Irish Examiner

"A classical storybook … exciting tales" The Kerryman

"An ode to traditional style children's storybooks" Kerry's Eye

"A delight to read … Refreshing" The Voice magazine

www.jerrymulvihill.com